Conception

a novel

by

Marie Garcia

Delta Files

The Hotel Slayings

The Masked Killer

Ballerina

Recreational Murder

Fake

Trea-Bella Donna

Vacay

Trea-Bella Donna: Prison Queen

Suicide Killer

State Route

Coroner

Addyson

Broken

Redemption

Addyson Private Investigations

Kaula Dawkins

Adam Corning

Pami Simpson

Untold Stories

Haden Delta, Volume 1

Tessa Kellogg

Chapter One

Vancouver, Washington
February 1, 1990

I looked up at my boyfriend adoringly. He was everything that I'd wanted in a boyfriend, potential husband, and future father for my children.

His name was James Kellogg. He was star of the baseball team, basketball team, debate team, and was the class president. James stood at 6-foot-5-inches tall and weighed about 220 pounds. He was lean, but built. Had blond hair and deep blue eyes.

James was also kind and caring. Always willing to help a friend, family member, or a stranger. He tutored the kids at school who needed it. Even the kids in middle school and elementary schools.

He wasn't freaked out that I had a fraternal twin brother, Terrence, either. A big plus. It's always seemed to freak out my previous boyfriends. Not that I understand why and not that there were a lot of them, but still.

Jamwa and I had been dating for about two years now and had only begun to be intimate in the last six months. We used condoms and I was on the pill. I had plans and aspirations. I didn't want or need a complication like that right now.

I was so happy.

So were my parents and that was saying something. It was very hard for me to make them happy. I kept my grades up and worked after school. I even volunteered. I was on the cheer squad, the captain no less. Nothing pleased them.

Not until I started dating James. I think they loved him more than they loved me. Terrence said I was crazy to think that, but that's how I felt.

Even my sisters commented on it. My brother,

too. Older brother, Troy. He was so annoying, he had commented on it.

* * *

"Addy?" James asked. "Honey? Addyson?"

"Huh?" I replied.

"You okay? You looked like you were a million miles away."

"Oh." I smiled up at him. "Yeah. I was thinking about that chem test on Friday."

"Mid-term. Gonna be rough."

I laughed.

"Addyson March!" He smiled. "Don't you laugh at me."

"You know you'll ace it. Chem is your best subject."

We were standing in line for lunch. Crappy food, but nice to be able to be together. We had nearly all of our classes together except gym and choir.

Gym, because they separated the girls and the guys; and choir because he couldn't carry a tune in a bucket with two lids on it.

As nice as it is to see each other all day long, it

was also nice to get a break from one another. I loved him, but he could be a bit much.

James stood behind me, arms wrapped around my waist, as we moved towards the head of the line. I could see Terrence already sitting at our table.

I waved at him and smiled.

"How's he doing?" James asked, suddenly somber.

"Good. Heartbroken."

"Not a good way to lose..."

"No." I pulled his arms tighter around me. "No, it's not."

Terrence and his long-time girlfriend, Tory Veroni, were in a head-on collision. Tory died on impact. She'd had her legs on the dashboard and had been folded in half. Essentially.

Terrence had been saved by his seat belt and the airbag. He was committed to a psych ward due to severe survivor's guilt. He was there for over a month. There are still nights where he wakes up, terrified.

I spend those nights with him. Much to the displeasure of my parents and my boyfriend. He would rather me spend them with him. Especially now that we were having sex.

"We're up," James said. "What do you want babe?"

"Fries and something to drink."

"Got it. Go have a seat."

"Thanks. Lots of ketchup."

He nodded and I went to sit with Terrence.

Chapter Two

"What's up, bro?" I said, sitting down.

He shrugged. "Worried about my math mid-term," he replied. 'Trig is not my strong suit."

"Mine either. Just hate math in general."

"What do you want to be when you grow up?"

I shrugged myself. "Hadn't really thought about it. Something where I don't have to go to college maybe?"

"Hey, all," a female voice said. "What's shakin'?"

I rolled my eyes and Terrence laughed. It was good to hear, he didn't laugh nearly as much anymore. "Hey, Hailey."

"Did you roll your eyes?"

I grinned. "Of course."

She growled. "If you weren't cute..."

I laughed. "Yeah, yeah. How was English?"

"Okay. Ms. Horowitz was on point today."

"Oh, boy."

"Yeah. She didn't let us get away with anything."

"Does she ever?"

Hailey laughed. "You have a point. She's a good teacher."

"She is."

Hailey sighed. "Here comes your boyfriend."

I looked up and James had our food and was on his way to the table. Hailey was the only one who didn't like James. I didn't understand it.

I know she liked me, but she knows that I like boys. There was nothing wrong with how she felt about girls or even about me. As long as they treated her well and she was happy that was all I cared about.

"Hi, Hailey," James said, setting my food down in front of me. "Got you an orange soda, that okay, babe?"

"Great. Thanks," I replied, happily. I loved orange soda. That or root beer worked for me.

"How's it going, Terrence?"

"All right. Dreading Trig," Terrence responded. "Advanced Chem, too."

"Both mid-terms area going to be brutal."

We all agreed with that statement.

* * *

That night, after cheer practice, there was a knock on my my bedroom door. "Come in," I called.

"Hey," Troy, my older brother, said. "Got a minute?"

"Sure." I set my pencil down. "What's up?"

"How's Terrence doing?"

"Good. He was worried about his Trig and Advanced Chem mid-terms. Why?"

"He doesn't talk a lot anymore. I'm his big brother. I worry."

I looked at Troy and he seemed sincere, but with him you never knew.

"Unless he starts talking about hurting himself,

I don't think we have to worry about him. He's kept his grades up and all of his after school activities. He's okay."

He thought about it for a minute and then nodded. "How are you?"

"All right."

"They on your case again?"

I gave a curt laugh. "When *aren't* they, Troy? I don't know what I've done to deserve how they treat me. I go to school. I'm on the student counsel, I volunteer. I'm captain of the cheer squad. I'm dating the most popular boy in school. I don't understand."

He came to stand beside my bed. "It's not you."

"Do you know something?"

He shook his head. "No. They are crazy, messed up people. They have issues and they are taking it out on you. Ignore them."

"That's easy for you to say. You don't get treated like I do. None of you do. Except Terrence. Once in awhile."

My brother looked at me. "I don't know what to say to that. You're right."

"There's nothing to say."

He nodded again and left my room.

Chapter Three

A couple of days later, Terrence knocked on my door before school.

"Got a second?" he asked.

"Sure," I said, gathering my books. "What's on your mind?"

"Do you think people will ever look at me the same way?"

"Of course." I looked at him. "It will take time. It was a terrible tragedy. Losing Terry the way you did. I don't think that she would want you to bury yourself with her. I know you are nowhere ready to even try, but you need to see your friends."

"I..."

I held my hands up. "Terrence, I know you spend time with them at school and at school functions, but you haven't seen anyone outside of school."

I had all of my things ready and started to leave my bedroom. Terrence followed.

"You haven't hung out with anyone since the accident. It's like you blamed everyone, but mostly yourself. I told Troy that you were okay a couple of days ago, but I started watching you. I started thinking back. You're not okay. Not completely."

"Addy..."

We got into the car that we shared and Terrence got into the passenger side while I slid into the driver's seat after putting my bags in the backseat.

I looked at him before I started the car. "Tell me that I'm wrong."

He sighed heavily. "I can't."

"I'm here for you. Always. Maybe talking to a shrink would help."

Terrence shrugged.

I sighed, started the car, and pulled away from

the house.

Terrence needed to help himself. He needed to want to help himself or he'd never get back to his old self.

* * *

The ride to school was silent. He was brooding. Deeply thinking about what I had told him. He wants to be better. Knows that he needs to be better.

I just don't think he knows how.

We pulled into the school and into our assigned spot. Terrence hopped out of the car, grabbed his book bag, and ran off. Probably to his locker.

I moved to open my door, but it opened as I put my hand on the handle.

"Hey, honey!" James exclaimed.

"Geez!" I said. "You scared me!"

"Sorry. I saw you pull in from my car. Everything okay? Terrence kind of bolted."

"Faced some hard truths this morning."

"Ah. Can I help with your bag?"

I smiled. "Sure."

He helped me out of the car and kissed me

before getting my things from the back of the car.

"How'd you sleep?"

"Hard."

I blushed. He laughed.

"What?"

"You're so cute when you're embarrassed."

"Shut up!" He laughed harder. So hard that he almost fell over.

I started laughing then myself.

"Mean."

"Never." I held out my hand and he took it, brushing his lips across my knuckles.

Not a bad way to start the morning and the day of mid-terms.

Chapter Four

It was lunch time and Terrence had not shown up to any of his classes and he wasn't at lunch.

"Babe, have you seen Terrence?" I asked. "He hasn't been in any of his classes. I checked with the office."

"No," James said.

"Hailey?"

She shook her head.

"I'm worried. I know he's here. I brought him."

"Did he bring his keys?"

"No. He hasn't driven since the accident. I'm going to the office. Again."

James nodded.

* * *

Ms. Judy looked up as the office door opened.

"Ms. March," she said.

"I know I asked already, but have you heard from Terrence?" I asked, again. "I know he's here. I brought him to school."

"He never showed up for his morning classes. Did he come for lunch?"

"No. I'm concerned."

"Let me call your parents. We'll find him."

"Can we call him on the PA system? Or see if security can go to the restrooms? Please, Ms. Judy?"

"I'll call Ralphie and Darnell to have them go look."

"You'll let me know?"

"Of course."

"Thank you, Ms. Judy."

We had that "twin thing" as many of our friends called it and it wasn't feeling well. There was something wrong. I just knew it.

"He'll be okay, dear."

I nodded and went back to my table.

"They haven't heard anything," I said, sitting. "They are calling our parents and Ms. Judy is going to ask Ralphie and Darnell to check the restrooms."

James nodded and took my hand. "Are you okay?" he asked.

I shook my head. "I'm seriously concerned."

"I thought he was okay."

"No. Not really."

"What can we do to help?"

"I don't know."

* * *

I was walking to my class after lunch and could see Ralphie and Darnell going through the restrooms. I was almost to class when I heard a scream.

I saw Ralphie running towards the office, speaking frantically into her walkie-talkie.

I dropped my bag and ran towards where Darnell was trying to keep the students out of the restroom.

He looked stricken.

Chapter Five

"Darnell?" I asked. "Is it Terrence?"

He nodded. "You can't..." he started.

I pushed passed him and fell to my knees beside my twin. Why was no one helping him?

There was blood coming from his wrists. I ripped my shirt and started wrapping his wrists as tightly as I could and checked his pulse. It was there and he was breathing. Barely.

"Darnell, hold his wrists so I can do CPR!"

"I can't," he called back. "I gotta keep the kids back!"

"Fuck that. He's gonna die!"

"I'll help," someone said.

"Please. Just hold his wrists to slow the bleeding."

"Sure."

I didn't recognize the student, but I was grateful.

Once he had a firm hold on Terrence's wrists; I moved to breathing air into his lungs. I didn't want to do chest compressions. It would just pump more blood out of his wrists.

"How long until an ambulance is here?"

I could Darnell calling the office on his walkie-talkie. "Five minutes."

"Hang on, Terrance. Don't leave me. Please stay with me."

I felt someone wrap something around my shoulders as I kept breathing into Terrance's mouth.

* * *

Someone started pulling me away.

"No!" I screamed.

"I'm an EMT, honey." the voice said. "Let us help."

I nodded and let the unnamed student pull me

away. He also wrapped a jacket around me since my shirt was wrapped around my brother's wrists.

There was a flurry of activity in the restroom.

"Are you his sister?" an officer asked.

"Yes," I replied.

"What happened?"

"I don't know. He's been depressed since his girlfriend died in a car accident. We had a talk about him isolating himself and needing help this morning. He jumped out of the car once I parked. He never showed up to any of his classes or lunch."

"Did you report it?"

"Yes. We have a couple of classes together; when he didn't show up to our second class I went to the office. Then when he didn't show up for lunch, I went back to the office. They sent security. I heard a scream. You know the rest."

"Did you think he'd do this?"

I shook my head. "Can I go with him?"

"Of course. We're moving him now. What about your parents?"

"The school was supposed to notify them when

we couldn't find him."

The officer nodded.

I heard the paramedics moving him to the gurney and then it being lifted up.

"His sister," the officer said. "She's going with."

"Let's move."

I rushed with them, picking up my forgotten book bag as we ran passed where I'd dropped it.

They loaded Terrance in the back of the ambulance and helped me in.

I was covered with blood from the knees down and it was all over the back of my arms and hands.

Please, Terrance, I prayed. *Don't leave me. I need you. Please. Please. Please.*

I kept repeating the last over and over again the entire ride to the hospital.

Chapter 6

I was sitting outside of the room where the doctors were working on Terrence. I was waiting on word from my parents. Waiting on word about Terrence.

No one would tell me anything. The nurses that were coming and going wouldn't look at me.

"Ms. March?" a male voice asked, gently.

I looked up into kind, blue eyes. "Yes?" I replied. "How is he?"

"Stable. We'll be keeping him for a couple of days. We'll be moving him upstairs to a room in the ICU. Where are your parents?"

I shrugged. "Can I see him? Please?"

He nodded. "He's not conscious."

"Okay."

I walked by the doctor and he stopped me by putting his hand on my shoulder. "Ms. March?"

"Yes?" I looked over my shoulder at him.

"Your brother is alive because of you. I don't know how long he'd been bleeding in that restroom, but he's alive because of you."

I nodded again, tears in my eyes and walked in to be with my brother.

* * *

He looked so small. Pale. There were angry, jagged scars down his wrists. They'd used to stitches to close them up.

Terrence was moved to room in the ICU a few hours later and there was still no word from our parents.

To hell with them.

There was a knock on the door and someone entered before I could say anything.

It was a nurse. They'd been coming and about every half an hour or so to check his vitals.

"Are you okay?" she asked.

"Fine," I replied. "Any word from my parents?"

"Not yet. Your boyfriend called. He wants to come get you."

"No."

"You need to eat, dear. Change. You can come back."

"No."

"Okay."

The nurse went about her business and I held Terrence's hand, cursing my parents for being who they were. Uncaring assholes.

* * *

About two hours after the nurse had left, I'd fallen asleep with my hand on the bed, holding Terrance's hand.

Someone was shaking my shoulder.

"Wake up, you little whore," a familiar female voice said.

"Sis, we brought you some clothes," a soft-familiar voice said.

"Thank you, Troy," I replied, groggily. "Mother."

"What happened?" she demanded.

"I wasn't with him when he did it. We arrived at school. He went into the building and didn't show up for his morning classes. Didn't show up for lunch. I reported it to the office twice. He was found after I reported him missing the second time by campus security."

"What happened?" a familiar male voice demanded.

"Father." I repeated everything that I'd just said to my brother and my mother.

"Where is your shirt?"

"That's what you ask? How about how your son is doing? To answer your question, I am wearing *most* of my shirt. I ripped the rest of it off to wrap his wrists to stop the bleeding. I wrapped them so he wouldn't die."

"What your tone, missy."

I looked to my mother and back again. "Do either of you care that one of your children is lying in that bed? That he nearly died today? Do you care that because you wouldn't let him get help that he tried to kill himself?"

"He is weak. Just like you are."

I glared at him. "We may be weak, but at least we care."

There was a knock on the door and the doctor entered the room. I ignored my parents. "How is he?"

"After he wake up, he will be transferred to the psych unit for observation," he replied. "He may need medication."

"How much is that going to cost?" my father demanded.

The doctor turned to look at him. "Your son needs help. You can't put a price on that. Would you rather bury him? A funeral costs more than that. Several thousand dollars."

"Asshole."

"Get out."

"You can't speak to me that way!"

"I can speak to you anyway I wish."

I stared at the doctor and my father. I tried to make myself as small as possible.

Chapter 7

February 5, 1990

I was sitting next to Terrence's bed when he finally opened his eyes.

"Addy?" he asked, groggily. His voice was a little hoarse, because of the tube that had been down his throat for about a day and a half. "What happened?"

"You were at school and tried to kill yourself," I replied. "Ralphie and Darnell found you. I gave you my shirt. I bound your wounds. I did mouth to mouth. Another student held your wrists."

"Oh, Addy…"

"Why?"

"It hurts without her."

"I understand that; however, you *lived*. You *survived*. I know that she wouldn't want this for you. She would want you to live."

Terrance did something that I'd never seen him do before. He cried.

"I'm sorry if our talk the other morning made you do this."

Terrence shook his head. "I was planning on it anyway. I loved her so much. I miss Terry. We will be together again."

"Yes, you will. Please, *don't* do that again Promise me."

He looked at me. "I won't."

"Good. You are strong. You will continue to be strong. You can and will honor Terry by living. By thriving."

He nodded. "Where are Mom and Dad?"

"The doctor won't let them come in."

Terrence was shocked. "What? Why?"

"The doctor didn't like that Dad seemed to care more about the cost of your treatments and possible medications than you."

"Oh."

"The doctor says you need to go to a psych hospital."

"Oh."

I nodded and took his hand.

* * *

An hour later, there was a knock on the door.

"You're awake," the doctor said. "Good. How are you feeling?"

"Okay," Terrence said. "Embarrassed."

"There is no need to be embarrassed, Terrence. These happen a lot. We're going to put you on some medication and then we're going to have you do an inpatient program for about a month and then an outpatient program for about a year."

Terrence nodded. "I'd rather just do the outpatient stuff and medication. I can't be away from school that long or my sister."

"Why?"

"I just need to be with her. Please? I will make sure that I'm at every appointment. I'll take all the pills that you want me to.”

The doctor thought about it. “Addyson, if you see any signs he's in a bad place, then you need to get him admitted. That's the only way I'll agree to it.”

“All right,” I replied.

“Terrence, I will hold you to what you said. You will attend every appointment set. Take every pill.”

“Yes, Doctor.”

“Fine. I want you to have more night for observation and then you can go home tomorrow.”

“Thank you.” The doctor nodded and left. “Addy, go home. Shower. Check in with James. Do homework.”

“I don't want to leave you.”

He took my hand. “I'll be okay.”

“I'll be back as soon as I can.”

Terrence kissed the back of my hand and I called James from his room.

Chapter 8

I'd allowed Hailey to come get my car keys and bring me mine and Terrence's car the previous day.

An hour later, I was sitting in front of James's house and took a second to breath deeply.

There was a knock on my window and I jumped. I looked up and it was James. I opened the door and stepped out, "Hey," I said.

"How is he?" James asked. "Are you okay?"

"He's awake and talking. Seems to be okay. I'm all right."

"So, what happened? There are a lot of rumors going around."

"Great." I closed the door and leaned against it.

"He was more depressed than I knew. Than anyone knew; really, and he tried to kill himself. He slit his wrists. He almost died. I used the bottom of my shirt to bind his wrists. Kept air flowing into his lungs."

"You tore your shirt?" He stared at me. "What were you thinking?"

I looked up at him. "That my brother, sorry, my *twin* brother was dying. That I didn't want to lose him."

Was he seriously asking me that question? What was wrong with him and my parents? My losing the bottom half of my shirt was nothing and would have been nothing compared to losing my brother.

"What about people seeing you without a shirt?"

"Who cares? If it had been you or Hailey or hell, a complete stranger, I would have done the same thing. Besides, it was just around my stomach. Nothing was exposed."

"But..."

"James, please? Just hold me?"

He looked at me like he wanted to argue, but something on my face must have changed his mind.

His face softened and he said, "Of course."

James took me into his arms and I melted into him. He was my safe place. My haven.

"I love you, James."

His arms tightened around me and he kissed the top of my head gently. "I love you, too, Addyson."

* * *

"I'm sorry," I said.

James pulled back and replied, "What do you mean? Was for?"

"For not being around the last few days."

"Don't worry about it. I understand."

"Glad *you* do."

"Your parents?"

"And my other siblings."

"Do you have time to come in?"

I nodded and he led me into the house.

"Hi, Mr. and Mrs. Simms," I said, as we entered the house.

"Hello, Addyson," his mother replied.

"Addyson," James's father said. "How are you doing?"

"I'm okay."

"Your family?"

"Okay."

"Sorry to hear about Terrence."

"Thank you."

"We'll be in my room," James said.

His parents nodded and went back to what they were doing.

Chapter 9

James closed the door and I sat down in the chair in front of his bed.

"So, what are they doing?" James asked. He took a seat on the bed.

"They don't seem to care what happened to Terrence. That he needs help. Literally, my dad demanded how much money his treatment would cost," I replied.

"Sheesh."

I got up and sat next to him. "The doctor kicked him—them—out. It's just been me with Terrance."

"Have you slept?"

"Not much and not well."

"I'll go to the living room. Take a nap."

I looked at him. "I can't stay long. He's getting out tomorrow. I'll sleep then."

"Will it help if I lay down with you?"

"Okay."

We laid back on the bed and he pulled me close to him. I closed my eyes and he held me tight.

* * *

When I woke up, I didn't know how much time had passed, but James was very happy to be pressed up behind me.

I rolled over to see him awake and looking at me. It was an expectant look. I smiled and kissed him.

He pulled me close and started kissing me back. His hands roamed all over my body. He cupped my breast through my top, teasing my nipple.

"Please," I begged.

Being with James was still so new. Being with a boy like this, period, was so new that I sometimes craved his touch. Especially when I was stressed out or worried. It helped clear my head.

James removed my top and bra. His mouth found my nipple, taut. He gently bit it and I gasped. He started to remove my pants and underwear and I let him.

I removed his pants and underwear; freeing his member.

"Please."

James positioned himself between my legs. He kissed me and slowly slid inside of me as I moaned silently into his mouth.

Chapter 10

After we cleaned up, James walked me to my car.

"Will you be at school tomorrow?" he asked.

"I don't know," I replied. "Probably not. Can you pick up my homework for me tomorrow and bring it by the house?"

"Of course."

We kissed and I got into my car. James closed my door, I waved, and drove off.

* * *

I pulled up to the hospital a short time later. I had just left home after showering and changing and tried to remember if I'd taken my birth control lately.

Did we use a condom just now?

I shrugged.

As I got out of my car, I saw Hailey a few cars over.

"Hey," I called out.

"Hey," she replied, walking over to me. "What's up?"

"Terrence is awake. Talking. I went home and showered. Changed. Listened to my family talk shit. Visited James."

"I see."

I looked at her, sideways. "Why do you hate James, Hailey?"

She shrugged. "I don't trust him, Addy. I don't know."

Then she was in front of me and pinned me to my car. "I love you, Addyson March."

I looked at her and my heart was pounding in my chest. I thought it was going to burst out of me.

My best friend did two things at once: she kissed me and slipped her hand into my pants. She found my clit and started rubbing it.

"I know that you don't do women. I know that, but I want to show you the sexuality of being with a woman." She spoke against my mouth. "Please, don't close your mind to it."

My breathing quickened. "Oh."

"Good girl."

My body shuddered.

"Come to my house tomorrow night. We need to talk."

"Okay."

She removed her fingers from my pants, looked at me while she licked her fingers, and said, "Yum."

Chapter 11

The next day, after Terrence was released from the hospital, and he was finally home, I made sure that he was all tucked in and resting before I called James.

"Hey, Mr. Simms?" I asked, when someone picked up.

"Hello," he replied. "Who is this?"

"It's Addyson, sir. Is James home?"

"No. He's out with the boys on a last minute camping trip for the weekend. He said he has your school work and will stop by on Monday. He also asked your teachers if they could extend both yours and Terrence's homework due dates. Said not to worry."

"Okay. Thank you."

I hung up and went to check on Terrence.

"Hey, Addy," he said.

"James has our homework and will bring it on Monday," I replied. "He went out of town. Camping trip."

"Okay."

"Would you be okay if I go out with Hailey for the night?"

"Sure. Go have fun."

I nodded and left.

* * *

I pulled up to Hailey's house and saw that only her car was in the driveway. I got out of the car and walked up to the door.

She opened the door before I could even knock on it.

"I saw you pull up," she said. "Thank you for coming."

"Sure," I replied. "Where are your parents?"

She shrugged. "You know they never tell me.

Could be gone for weeks."

I walked into the house and then into the living room. "You wanted to talk?"

"Yeah. I've been talking to the girls who used to date James."

"Okay."

"He gets abusive. Once he is told no. Once they get intimate."

"I've heard the rumors. We all have."

"He rapes them."

"Hailey..."

"See me, too. No one needs to know. Start telling him no. let me show you. Please?"

"Show me what?"

"This."

Hailey kissed me again and leaned me back against the couch. She kissed her way down to my neck and pulled back long enough to pull off my shirt and my bra.

She took my breast into her mouth and sucked my nipple taut. Hard. She rolled it around in her mouth and I threw my head back. Then she moved to the other and repeated what she'd done to the other one.

As she moved down my body, Hailey removed my pants and underwear in one move. Then she kissed me down there.

Hailey ran her tongue over and over my clit. Her fingers darted in and out of my opening. My hips moved against her.

"Oh, God. Oh, God. Oh, God."

She pulled something from underneath the cushion and slid it into me.

"Oh, God."

"Good girl. Louder. Feel it. Good girl."

"OH, GOD!"

It found my special spot and I screamed her name. Hailey caught it by kissing me.

She pulled me off the couch. "My turn," she said.

"I've never done this before," I replied.

"It's okay."

She moved my head to her breast and I did what she'd done to me. She moaned. "Good girl.

Again."

I repeated what I'd done. "Oh, good girl."

Then she pushed my head down her body until her vagina was in my face.

"Lick."

I did. Her hands held my head as I licked her from top to bottom.

"Good girl. Don't stop."

I did just as she'd done.

"Good girl. Good girl."

Chapter 12

Hailey made us dinner.

"Will you stay tonight?" she asked.

"Let me check on Terrence," I said.

"Of course."

I went to her phone and called my house. "Hello?" my father answered.

"He's sleeping. Where are you?"

"At Hailey's. May I stay tonight? Or the weekend?"

"Fine. Fine.

"I'll call tomorrow."

"Whatever."

He hung up. "Asshole."

"Terrence okay."

"Sleeping."

"Come finish dinner."

I nodded and dutifully took my seat at the table.

She slid beneath the table and I only had a second to wonder what she was going to do.

* * *

Vancouver, Washington

February 9, 1990

"I have to go home," I said.

Haily sighed and rolled over in her bed. "Thank you," she replied. "I've wanted to do this with you for a long time."

"No one will know."

"Not if you don't want them to."

"No."

"Then they won't. If you want to do this again you know where to find me."

I kissed her, got out of her bed, and got dressed.

What we'd done was fun, but it could never
happen again. It would never happen again.

Chapter 13

James should be home by now, so I drove to his house. I knocked on his front door and his Dad answered, "Addyson?" he asked.

"Is James home?" I asked.

"He's in his room."

"May I go?"

"Of course."

He moved so that I could walk into the house and closed the door behind me.

I went down the hall to James's room and knocked on the door. "Come in," he called.

* * *

"Hey," I said, entering his room. "How was your

camping trip?"

"Hey!" he exclaimed. "It was okay. We went up to Long Beach. Nothing happening up there. How's Terrence?"

"Okay, I guess. I spent the weekend with Hailey. Terrence said he was okay with it. I think he's seen too much of me and needed a breather. Time to think."

"How do you feel?"

"Good. I just left her place and wasn't quite ready to go home yet. I thought you might be back; well, I'd hoped you would be, so I came here."

"Works for me. Yours and Terrence's homework is on the bed. All the teachers gave you both two weeks' extensions on all the work and projects and tests."

I walked over and sat on his lap. "Thank you."

James wrapped his arms around me. "Any time."

I turned so that I straddled him. "I missed you."

"How much?"

I reached between us and freed him. I moved

my hand up and down a couple of times and he was hard. Ready to go. I stepped off of him and removed my pants and underwear. Pulled off my shirt and bra and straddled him again.

I used my hand to guide him in and moaned as he entered me.

"What?"

I stopped his questions by kissing him.

Chapter 14

James looked at him after I cleaned up.

"Are you okay?" he asked.

I smiled. "Great," I replied.

He studied me a bit longer and shrugged. "All right. Let me help you get the homework to your car. Are you coming back to school?"

"Tomorrow or the next day."

He smiled. "Good, we miss you."

"What has the school itself been saying about what happened to Terrence?"

"An attack. Someone found a way to get onto the school grounds."

"Okay. Better than what actually happened.

The real reason."

James looked at me. "What happened in that restroom?"

We gathered the books and worksheets and I didn't answer until we out by the car.

"You know what happened."

"You said that you tore your shirt."

I nodded. "I'd torn the bottom half of my shirt off and used those pieces to try and bind his wounds. I was still completely covered on the top. There was a student that stepped up when Darnell wouldn't help me."

"What about the dude?"

"Don't know him. I begged Darnell to help me, like I said, but he had to keep the other students out. This guy offered to help me and I wasn't about to let Terrence die, James."

"I get that, but what did that guy want?"

I stared at him. "Nothing. I didn't even get his name."

"But..."

"No." I put my things in the car and got in. "I'm

not doing this."

"Don't."

I shook my head and closed the door, and left.

Chapter 15

February 14, 1990

Vancouver, Washington

"Have you talked to James?" Terrence asked, as we pulled into the school.

"No," I replied, looking for a spot. "Mother is pissed. I don't exactly care."

"I know. Why aren't you speaking to him?"

I shrugged. "It just seemed like he was more interested in the dude that was helping me and the fact that I used my shirt to save you than the fact that you were dying. It pissed me off."

"Addy..."

I shook my head as I found a spot and pulled

in. "It's not okay, Terrence."

"You'll have to talk to him today."

"I don't have to do anything. He was not in the right here."

Terrence put his hand on my shoulder and I looked at him. "That's not what I meant. Sis, you have classes with him. HE's your partner on all your projects."

"I know, but that's going to change."

"What do you mean?"

"I mean that maybe it's time to start distancing myself from him. He may be too jealous. Too controlling."

"Is he hitting you?"

"No, but if I can't help you without him getting jealous then what's he gonna do when I become a cop?"

"You still want to do that?"

"Of course. It's all I've wanted to do."

Terrence smiled. "I know. You'll be a great one, too."

"So will you."

He nodded and then looked out the window behind me. "We have company."

"James?"

"Yep. Need me to stay?"

"No. I'll be okay."

"Okay."

Terrence got out of the car and I saw James come around and get in.

"Are you fucking another guy? What did you do at the hospital?" he demanded.

"You need to watch your tone with me, and get out of my car," I said, calmly.

I grabbed my book bag and he grabbed my arm and held it tightly enough that I would be bruised later. "You listen to me you whore," he said, his voice very harsh. "You *will* watch your tone with *me. You* belong to me. Your parents sold you to me. They hate you. They want you gone."

My eyes burned and my heart hurt. "Let go of me. I. Do. Not. Belong. To. Anyone."

I pulled my arm free, finished grabbing my things, and got out of my car. Afraid of James for the first time.

* * *

When I got to my first class, I sat between two classmates, and fought not to cry.

They looked shocked, but didn't say anything.

I could feel Hailey's eyes o me. I could feel Terrence's eyes on me, and worst of all, I could feel James's eyes on me.

I put my head down, opened my book, and ignored everything.

Chapter 16

Hailey pulled me into the nearest girls' room. She checked to make sure we were alone.

"What's wrong?" she demanded.

She'd grabbed the arm that James had earlier and I winced. Hailey pulled my jacket off and gasped.

"What happened?"

"Nothing," I said, pulling my jacket back on. "Don't worry about it."

"Addy..."

"Don't. Please."

I felt tears begin to well up and I didn't want to cry at school.

"I'm here."

I nodded and splashed some water on my face.

* * *

I made it through the rest of the day without having to see James and I was grateful for that.

Terrence was at practice, so I went home by myself. James was waiting for me.

"Get in the fucking car and don't speak," he threatened. "I will fucking kill you, if you speak."

I glanced at my house.

"Don't think about screaming. It will be much worse if you scream."

I got into the car and buckled up.

James drove us out to the woods and shut the car off.

"Why have you been avoiding me all day? Are you fucking the dude from the restroom?" James demanded.

"You are acting jealous for no reason," I said. "I don't even know the dude from the restroom's name."

"Lying bitch!"

He backhanded me. I unbuckled my seat belt and crawled into the backseat. He grabbed my pants and ripped them.

"You're mine! You're mine!"

"No! James, stop!"

He punched me. "Shut up. Bitch! Cunt!"

James ripped my panties off and tossed them into the front seat. He forced me to turn over and he shoved his fingers into me; hard and fast.

"Stop! Stop!"

"You like that? I saw you with that lesbian whore!"

"No! Stop!" I started crying and I felt him trying to shove his fist into me. I started screaming. "No! No!"

"Scream, baby, scream!"

Finally, he pulled his pants down and his boxers. I tried to back away and open the door, but he punched me in the face.

James entered me and didn't stop.

Chapter 17

James put his pants and stuff on before crawling into the front seat.

"Stay there you, bitch," he ordered. He drove us out of the woods and it looked we ended up at a gas station.

"Stay down."

I didn't move. I was too hurt and too scared to move. He didn't even bother to cover me up. I was exposed to anyone who would walk by.

Distantly, I could hear him on the phone.

He was talking to someone that he and I would be camping for a couple of days, so not to worry.

James came back to the car and grabbed his

wallet before going into the gas station.

* * *

A short time later, he returned with a bag of numerous items.

He started the car and returned to the woods.

James yanked me out of the car and threw me to the ground. He went to his trunk and pulled out a tent.

"Move or it's gonna get worse," he said.

"How could it get worse, James?" I asked, numbly. "You just beat me. Raped me."

"I did no such thing."

I dared not to look at him.

He really didn't think he'd just done those things to me?

James set up the tent and tossed a large sleeping bag inside. "Get in."

I slowly crawled inside and he was right behind me.

"Please, don't," I begged.

"You like it. I saw you with Hailey."

He pulled his pants down again and rammed

himself into my anus.

Chapter 18

February 17, 1990
Vancouver, Washington

He, James, took my to my house and threw me out. "Don't say a word," he ordered.

I crawled to Terrence's window and he looked out. "Addy?" he asked.

"Help," I whispered.

"Mom! Call for help! Call 911!"

He jumped out the window, yanking the curtain off once he realized I had no clothes on.

* * *

My parents demanded to know what happened,

but I refused to say anything. Terrence stayed by my side, but I flinched whenever a man touched me.

The nurses called for a rape kit and a female doctor.

"Who did this to you?" my father demanded. He actually sounded concerned. I should have known better.

"James Kellogg," I croaked. I was barely able to speak. "James Kellogg."

"You're a liar," my mother said. "He's such a good boy."

"He did this, Mother."

My father shook his head. "He called us on Valentine's Day. Said you'd broken up with him, so you two would be camping. You know, so you could work it out. Said not to worry. Liar."

"Get out."

The nurse pushed them out of the door.

"I'm so sorry, honey," she said, gently. "The police are on their way."

I shook my head. "It's no use. It's no use."

"He should be reported," Terrence yelled.

"He's the golden boy. If my parents don't believe me, why would they?"

"Addy, you have to have faith in the justice system. If you don't, then how can you become a cop?"

"Do the rape kit, but I know the statistics, Terrence."

"You need to leave the room."

"I'll be right outside."

I nodded, not trusting myself to speak.

"It'll be okay honey," the nurse said.

"Okay."

"We'll explain every step, okay?" the doctor said.

"Okay."

She began and I cried the whole time.

Chapter 19

The police arrived while I was being examined.

"The police are here, honey," the nurse said. "Even if they might not believe you, you need to tell them what happened. It will help."

I sighed. "Okay, but please keep my brother out," I replied. "Just until they leave."

"Of course."

"Officer, she'll see you." She put her hand up and shook her head. "Just the officer."

* * *

"Can you tell me what happened?" the female officer asked. "Take you time. Please be as detailed as possible."

"I left school at three o' clock the day. Valentine's Day. My brother, Terrence, had practice so I went home alone. When I got home he was waiting. Told me to get in or he'd kill me. We drove to the woods and he demanded why I'd been avoiding him all day. He thought I was sleeping with someone else."

"Who?"

"A boy who helped me save my brother's life. I don't even know his name."

"Okay."

"I told him why I'd been avoiding him and that I didn't even know the name of the boy who'd helped me. He backhanded me. I crawled into the backseat to try and get away."

"What happened?"

"He ripped my pants off. Yelled that I was his. I begged him to stop. I told him no. He punched me and ripped my panties off." The tears started and the nurse took my hand. "He shoved his fingers into me. Said that I liked it. That he'd seen me with that lesbian whore."

I took a breath. "Do you need a minute?"

"No. He tried shoving his fist into me. Said that I should scream. I kept begging him to stop and telling him no. That's when he took his pants off and boxers off and he put his penis into me. I tried to get away again, but he punched me in the face. When he finished, he put his clothes back on, and we left. Went to a gas station.

"He told me to stay down, but he didn't bother to cover me up."

"What did he do at the gas station? Do you know which one?"

"I heard only bits and pieces. He called my home to tell my parents that we were going camping. My father said that he'd told them that I'd broken up with him and he wanted to take me camping so that we could work it out."

"Her father did say that when they showed up," the nurse agreed.

"Do you what time and which gas station?"

"No, ma'am. I was so scared that I didn't move. Once he was done on the phone, he returned to the car and grabbed his wallet. He left again and returned after he'd bought some things. We returned to the woods and he threw me out of the car. Then he put up a tent and raped me all weekend."

"Who? Did you actually break up with him?"

"No I was planning on it. Or just on getting some distance for a bit."

"Who?"

"James Kellogg."

"Oh."

"Yep."

The officer just looked at me.

Chapter 20

March 18, 1990

They had kept me in the hospital for a week while my body healed up.

My parents, surprise, surprise, sided with James. The officer I'd spoken with did believe me, but her superiors didn't. I knew it had been a waste of time.

Today, I was with Hailey after school. I hadn't been feeling well and didn't want to go home yet. Wasn't ready to be ridiculed and called a liar, which had become a daily event the last month.

"How are you?" Hailey asked, handing me a Sprite.

"Stomach is upset," I replied, taking the can of soda. "Been super emotional."

"Completely understandable."

I took a sip and it tasted terrible. Still wanted to puke. "Ugh."

Hailey looked at me. "Are you sure it's nothing else?"

"What do you mean?"

"Could you be pregnant?"

"N...oh no!"

"Let me go to the store."

I couldn't be pregnant. Not by James. Not by anyone. My parents were going to kill me.

* * *

"You're pregnant," Hailey said. "I'm so sorry. What are you going to do?"

"Go to the doctor and confirm it," I said. "These things can be wrong. I'm not going to worry until then. Don't say anything."

"What about James?"

"What about him?"

"Are you going to tell him?"

"No."

"Why not?"

I looked at her then. "Really?"

Chapter 21

March 24, 1990

Portland, Oregon

"Do you have a parent or guardian with you?" the nurse asked.

"No," I replied. "Please, I need a pregnancy test. I was raped and it might be my rapist's baby. I don't want to say anything until I know."

"All right, honey. Follow me."

I followed her into an examining room and she asked me some questions. "The doctor will be in soon."

I nodded and waited for the doctor.

* * *

"Can you tell me what brings you here today?" the doctor asked, as she walked in.

"I was raped a month ago," I said. "He was my boyfriend prior, but it had to have happened on Valentine's Day."

"Oh my. Well, lay back and we'll check."

I nodded and the nurse helped me lay back and get situated on the exam table.

"We're going to insert the ultrasound inside. If you are pregnant, you're still early enough that it won't show up on a regular ultrasound. There will be a bit of pressure."

I took a deep breath. "Okay."

"Ready?"

"Yes."

She carefully inserted the want and turned on the machine.

"Okay." She moved it around. "You are pregnant. About four weeks. You can see the egg sac and the baby here. It's small, but there."

I refused to look. "No, no, no."

"I'm so sorry. We'll give you a few minutes and

the nurse will help you."

"No, no, no."

I felt like I'd been violated all over again.

Chapter 22

April 26, 1990

Vancouver, Washington

I was starting to show and there was no denying it any longer. I couldn't keep it from my parents anymore.

Hailey had helped me feel comfortable with sex again. She'd been kind and gentle with me. Patient. Then she started to distance herself from me and began hanging out with James. They had become as thick as thieves.

"Addy?" Terrence asked. "Are you okay?"

"No," I replied.

We were at lunch and I looked away from where

Hailey was hanging all over James. I pushed my food away, disgusted.

"What's wrong?"

"I'll tell you later."

He looked over to Hailey and James. "Are you jealous?"

I shook my head. "Disgusted."

"Want to leave?"

"Please. I'm done with school."

We got up and left.

"Where to?"

I shrugged. "Anywhere but home."

"Let's get a burger or something."

"You can. Grab it and let's go to the park."

"Sure."

I drove to the closest burger place and ordered him what he wanted, paid, and drove to the park. The smell of the burger was making me sick, so I rolled the windows down.

I parked and we got out and walked to the picnic tables.

"I'm pregnant, Terrence," I said. "It's James's

baby and I don't know what to do. I'm scared, I'm about eight weeks.”

“What?” he replied.

I looked at him. “You're going to be an uncle.”

“Are you okay?”

“No.” I started crying. “I don't want an abortion. I want to keep the baby.”

“Addy…”

“I'm scared that James will find out and hurt me. I'm scared that when Mother and Father find out that they'll kick me out.”

“What? I won't let that happen.”

I smiled. “You can't stop it.”

He hugged me. “I got you.”

“Thanks.”

Chapter 23

"Mother? Father?" I said, as Terrence and I walked in. "May I speak with you?"

"You little whore!" my father bellowed.

Terrence stepped in front of me.

"Get in here you little bitch," my mother added.

He kept himself in front of me and we walked into the living room. Standing there were James, Hailey, and James's parents.

"You fucked him," James's father said. "You accused him of rape, falsely. Now you are pregnant?"

"Wha..." I started.

"Don't deny it," James's mother said.

Hailey stepped forward and produced a

pregnancy test. "I'm sorry," she said.

I glared at her from around Terrence. "Liar."

"Why didn't you tell me?" James asked.

"You raped me."

"No, I didn't. It was consensual."

"Was the beating consensual as well?"

"I never hit you. You fell in the woods."

"You are leaving tonight," my mother said. "You will keep the pregnancy and put the baby up for adoption."

Terrence took a step towards James and I stopped him. "I want to keep my baby."

"No. If you do you will leave," my father said.

"No," Terrence said.

"No," Terrence said.

"Fine. James told me that you hated me. He told me that you wanted me gone. That you'd sold me to him. I'll keep my baby and leave."

My father glared at me and backhanded me. "You cunt. You will give that child up. You will do as we say."

"Addy..."

I looked at Terrence and he looked terrified.

"Please."

I nodded.

"Help her pack, Terrence. We will have the car ready. Thirty minutes."

Terrence and I walked up the stairs to my room and I glanced back at James. He was grinning.

* * *

Neither of my parents spoke to me as we drove through the night to some small town in Idaho.

Terrence was not with us as he had to stay to take care of our younger siblings.

I slept, briefly on the drive.

"We're here," my mother said.

"Get out," my father said. "They will call after you deliver and the child is gone. We'll come and get you then."

"You aren't coming in?" I asked. Really not surprised.

"No," my mother said.

"Don't call. Don't write. Don't reach out."

"But..."

"No, buts. Get out."

I grabbed the bag that I'd packed with Terrence's help. Pictures of the two of us, clothes. Books.

I got out and the second I closed the door, they drove off.

Chapter 24

I walked into the building and was greeted by a young woman.

"Hello, welcome to *Talia's Home for Girls*," she said. "How may I help you?"

"My name is Addyson March and my parents just dropped me off," I said.

"Okay." She pulled out a folder and looked at it. "Oh."

"Can I ask a question?"

"Of course."

"Do I have to give my baby up? Can I stay until birth and then leave?"

"Do you want your baby?"

"Yes."

"It says you are here, because you don't want to keep the baby."

"No, ma'am. I want my baby. My parents, my ex-boyfriend, and his parents are forcing me."

"Well, you'll talk to one of our intake counselors about all of that."

"All right."

"Where are your parents? There's paperwork to sign."

I looked around, embarrassed. "They left."

"Oh." She looked unsure of what to do. "Well, let's get you to a room and the counselor will come in and speak with you soon. Breakfast is at seven o'clock in the morning. Lunch is at noon. Dinner is at seven o'clock in the evening. You'll be expected to attend birthing classes as well as regular school classes."

"Okay."

"Follow me."

I still held my bag and followed her down the hall.

"We're her. This is your room. You'll have a

private room."

"Okay."

"The counselor will be in shortly."

I nodded and was left alone in a strange town in a strange room. I hated my parents. I hated James. I hated his parents. I hated Hailey.

There was a knock on the door.

"Come in," I said.

"My name is Geneva," the middle aged woman said. "I'm one of the intake counselors here. May I sit?"

"Sure."

I took a seat on the bed and crossed my legs.

"There wasn't a lot in the file. Can you tell me why you don't want your baby? How far along are you?"

I sighed loudly. "So, I was beaten and raped by my ex-boyfriend. He raped and beat me over the course of a weekend back in February. I found out I was pregnant a month later and when I went to tell my parents last night. My ex-boyfriend and ex-best friend had beaten me to the punch."

"The bruise?"

"My father backhanded me."

"Oh."

"I know that they baby is the result of a rape, but I want my baby."

"That won't happen."

"What? Why?"

"Your parents have paid extra to make sure you don't keep the baby."

I stared. "What?"

"Unfortunately, you have no choice. Your ex-boyfriend will also be here when you deliver."

"No."

"Yes. Again, they paid extra."

I started to cry.

Chapter 25

November 5, 1990

Nampa, Idaho

"Keep him away from me!" I yelled.

"Baby!" James started.

"No!"

"Miss…" the nurse said.

"Please. Keep him away!"

"Out."

"The money…"

"Screw the money! Get out!"

James stalked out of the room and the nurse closed the door. "Remember your breathing. In and hold...two...three...four. Good. In and out...two...three...four."

The doctor came in. "The people who are adopting your baby are outside, waiting," she said. "They don't want you to hold the baby."

"What?"

"I'm sorry, Addyson."

"Can you tel me if it's a boy or a girl, at least?"

I'd opted to wait until birth to find out what I was having.

"Yes."

I screamed as a contraction rocked my body.

"Push on the next contraction. You're finally dilated."

"Okay."

I hated my parents. I hated the Kellogg family. I hoped that I never saw any of them again.

"Push."

I did with all my might. It took maybe, twenty minutes more of pushing. "It's a girl."

Chapter 26

They took her away and I started crying.

"My baby! My baby!" I screamed. "Please!"

James came in, grinning. "You'll never see her again," he sneered. "Bitch. You deserve this. I *did* rape you. Cunt. I'd do it again."

"Give me my baby!"

"No. My parents are adopting her as part of the agreement with your parents."

I screamed and tried to get up.

The doctor held me down. "I'm so sorry, Addyson," she said. "I'm so sorry."

I turned my head from the door and cried while they cleaned me up and mourned the loss of my daughter.

"What's her name?" the nurse asked.

"Tessa."

"Beautiful."

I nodded and hoped the pain would end.

* * *

Two days later, I was back home and my parents were worse than ever.

"Are yo okay, Addy?" Terrence asked.

"No," I replied, voice lifeless. Toneless. "I hate them."

"Addy..."

I looked at Terence. "Are you defending them?"

"No."

"They let my rapist's parents adopt my baby girl. They made sure that I would never see her again. They made sure I wouldn't even get to hold her after she was born."

"Oh, Addy..."

"I hate them."

Terrence nodded.

"The feeling is mutual," my mother said.

"Leave me alone," I said.

"Soon, whore."

"Don't think of looking for your little bastard either," my father said. "Or trying to run into the Kellogg's."

"Why not?"

"Because they moved away."

My parents sneered at me. Such evil smiles they wore.

I got up and went to my room, closing the door so I didn't have to hear them laughing.

Chapter 27

November 12, 1990
Vancouver, Washington

Terrence was at school and had taken the car. He'd asked me if I'd wanted it and I'd told him that I'd be okay. Once he left; however, my parents became relentless.

I left and caught the bus.

When I got to the mall, I called the school and sent a message to Terrence that I was at the mall and to pick me up when he was done.

I was sitting in the food court scarfing down cheese fries when someone stopped at my table.

"Excuse me," a deep male voice said. "May I sit down?"

I looked up. "Sure," I said.

"I don't know if you remember me or not." He sat down.

"You're the one who helped me with my brother."

"Yes. I'm glad he's doing better."

"Much. Thank you. I'm Addyson March. Terrence is my twin brother."

"Barry Hardy. I just moved here from Seattle. Well, about ten months ago."

"That's why I didn't recognize you! I've been in the same school district with the same kids since kindergarten. I was raised with most of my classmates."

"Ah. Where have you been?"

I shook my head. "I'd rather not talk about it, if you don't mind?"

"Sure. Sure."

"Thank you for helping with my brother. He'd have died if you hadn't helped me."

"You're welcome, but I don't believe that to be true."

"Why aren't you in school?"

"Why aren't you?

"It's hard to trust right now."

Barry looked at me. "You can trust me, Addyson."

"I've been hurt."

"I won't hurt you."

I looked at him and I don't know why, but I felt safe. "You'll regret asking."

"Do you see me running away?"

"Not yet."

"Try me."

I signed and looked at him square in the face. "Okay, but don't say I didn't warn you."

He nodded. "Consider me warned."

Chapter 28

"My boyfriend; ex-boyfriend, James kidnapped me, beat me, and raped me," I said, voice quiet and toneless. "He was convinced that you and I had hooked up. He became so jealous over nothing. The day I told him that I needed some space he managed to beat me home and dared me, basically, not to get in his car."

"What do you mean?" Barry asked.

"Said he'd kill me if I made a sound. I think he was hoping I didn't get into the car."

"Okay. Continue."

I nodded. "He drove me to the woods and demanded answered. I reported that there was nothing between us and that I didn't even know your name. Then he backhanded me."

Barry started to reach for my hand, but I pulled it away. He stopped and pulled his hand back.

"I crawled into the backseat. He beat me. Raped me. Took me; naked, to a nearby gas station. He called my parents and told them we were camping."

"What happened?"

I looked at him. "He beat and raped me over the next three days. I was tossed into my yard, naked. Hospitalized for a week."

I saw the looks of horror and rage on his face. Then pity; no, sorrow. Hatred even.

"So, is that why you haven't been in school? Is that why James hasn't been in school?"

I shook my head. "I got pregnant. I hadn't told my family right away. I'd told my friend, Hailey. She, in turn, told James. Kept the pregnancy test that I'd taken at her house."

"Oh, my."

"I told Terrence first. We went home so that I could tell my parents and James beat me to it. That night they drove me to Idaho and dropped me off. I told them that I wanted to keep my baby. My parents paid extra to take it way. James had his parents adopt her. They moved away."

Barry did grab my hand then and I didn't pull away. It was hard to be touched still.

"I never got to hold her. They just took her away. James came in, holding her, and admitted that he'd beaten me. Raped me. Said that he'd do it again."

"Oh..."

"Addyson?" a male voice asked.

"Hey, Terrence," I said.

"Are you ready? Is this dude bothering you?"

I shook my head. "This is Barry Hardy. He's the one who helped me save you."

"Oh! Thanks dude." Terrence stuck his hand out and Barry shook it. "Wish I could have thanked you earlier."

"No problem," Barry said. "There wasn't much time to introduce myself, ya know?"

"No problem. What's going on here?"

"Just talking."

"Ready to go home?"

"Sure." I stood up and looked down at Barry.
"Thank you."

"See you around."

I nodded and we left.

Chapter 29

Terrence led the way to the car. He'd parked just out of the food court of the mall.

"Is that a good idea?" he asked, as we exited the building.

"What do you mean?" I asked.

"Getting involved with someone else?"

I shook my head. "We aren't involved, Terrence. Not even close. We just met."

"What were you talking about?"

"What happened?"

"Why?"

I shrugged. "I needed to talk to someone."

"Addy, you can talk to me. Any time. You know that."

I waited while he opened the car. "I know, but I can't."

"Why not?"

He unlocked the doors and I got in.

"Let's go to the park. I don't wanna go home yet."

"Sure."

We drove the short distance to the park in silence. Once there we got out and went to the covered area. "Why not?" he asked, again.

"Because I don't want to upset you. We share everything, I know, but this I just can't. I want to. It's so difficult."

"How come?"

I shrugged. "I wouldn't want what happened to me to happen to anyone. I wouldn't want anyone to know what it feels like. To have the memory of it. Besides, you would try to find James and I can't lose you. I need you; now, more than ever."

"Okay." He slowly around my shoulders. "I need you, too."

I put my head on his shoulder. "I think that I'm

going to try and get emancipated. I need to get out of that house."

"Are you sure?"

I looked up at him. "I already have a job and a place to live. A car that they can't take away from me."

"When did you do all that?"

"While in Idaho. I spoke to a lawyer who specializes in emancipation. He knew of some places that would rent to me."

"I'll support you."

"I know."

"They'll cut you out."

"Already have."

"What about school?"

"I have enough credits to graduate. Thanks to being in Idaho."

"Okay."

"Do it with me."

"Of course."

"You can get your GED and we can graduate together."

He smiled. "Sounds good."

* * *

January 11, 1991

Terrence and I completed all of the requirements necessary to get emancipated. We had stable jobs, means to get around, to support ourselves, and we were both graduating early.

After we'd spoken back before Thanksgiving last year Terrence looked into his credits and found out that, because of all the electives he'd taken and extra classes that he'd taken, he'd be able to graduate with me without needing to get his GED.

Since we'd completed all of the regular classes, we only attended a two hour long study hall on the morning before work.

Our parents had no objects to letting us move out. Oddly, they let us keep the car. So, now Terrence and I each had a car in case we needed to get to work at different times.

Things were good.

Chapter 30

"Clean up, Aisle 1," I called.

I'd taken a job at the local department store. A little girl had spilled her slushie all over.

"I want another one!" she whined, her mother looked embarrassed.

"Of course. Three dollars," the clerk said.

I pulled the money out of my pocket. "Keep the two bucks."

The clerk smiled.

* * *

"Need a ride, good-looking?" a male voice asked.

I smiled and turned around. "Hey, Barry," I said. "No. I got the car tonight since I had to close.

What's up?"

"Just driving around. Enjoying the start of summer. The end of school."

"I hear that."

"You haven't been to school."

I smiled. "Terrence and I had enough credits to graduate and so we got emancipated."

"That must have been difficult."

I shrugged. "After what my parents did to me, it seemed fitting."

"That's true enough."

"See you later?"

"You bet."

I got in my car and drove off.

Chapter 31

June 18, 1991

Vancouver, Washington

There was a knock on my front door. I looked through the peephole and was shocked.

I opened the door and said, "How did you find out me and what the fuck do you want?"

"You have no reason to talk to me," Hailey began. "I..."

"Do you know what he did to me? Do you care? Do you have any idea what it was like?"

"No."

"I never got to hold my baby. They cut her cord

and handed her off to *his* parents. He came back and *admitted* what he had done."

"Ad..."

"No. Shut up. I never want to see you again, Hailey. When she was taken away from me I felt like I'd been raped again. Lose my address. Lose my phone number."

"Addy..."

"He beat you?"

"No."

"Raped you?"

"No."

"You fucked?"

"Yes."

"Did he knock you up? Take *your* child away?"

"No. No."

"Were you actually a lesbian? Did you really like me? Love me? Or was it really *him* that you wanted?"

"I thought I was. I like girls more than boys. Yes. Yes. No."

"Then there is nothing left to say. Goodbye,

Hailey. Have a great life."

I closed the door in her face and ignored the knocks on the door. If she kept it up, I would call the police, and have her removed.

* * *

Terrence was working late. He had two jobs. One was at a bookstore and the other was at a movie theater. He loved both jobs.

Unfortunately, we both were upset to find out that you had to be at least twenty-one to enroll in the police academy.

Anyway, I was feeling lonely. So, I decided to call Barry. I wasn't sure about having a male over, because of what had happened to me, so I thought maybe he'd be up for a movie.

"Hello?" he asked, answering on the second ring.

"Hey, Barry," I said. "It's Addyson. I'm a little bored and needing someone to hang out with. Would you like to go to a movie? We can meet at the theater and pick whatever is starting."

"Sure. I could pick you up at home."

"I'm not quite ready to be alone with a guy yet."

"Understandable. Which theater?" I told him.

"Okay. Meet you there in half an hour."

"Sure. Sounds good."

I hung up and got changed.

Chapter 32

I arrived first and parked near the front of the building. At least, as close as I could, and made sure to park underneath a streetlight.

Safety first.

Terrence was at the ticket booth.

"Hey, Addy!" he exclaimed. "What are you doing here?"

"Got lonely," I replied. "I called Barry to meet me here."

"A date?"

"Not exactly. I just didn't want to be alone."

"Okay. What movie?"

I shrugged. "We were gonna decide on what was going to be starting soon. Anything good."

"*Soapdish* is pretty funny. *My Girl.*"

"*My Girl.*"

"Here you go." He printed two tickets and slipped them through to me.

"Thanks."

He smiled. "Sure. Here comes Barry now."

I nodded and turned. "Hey," I said.

"Hi," he replied, smiling. "Pick something?"

"*My Girl.*"

"Sounds fun. Do you want popcorn?"

"Sure."

I waved to Terrence and we entered the building.

Barry bought some popcorn and drinks. Even some nachos.

* * *

"Thank you," I said, as we exited the theater.

"For what?" he replied.

"Being patient. Not pressuring me."

"Oh, sure."

"Sad movie."

He nodded. "It was good though. I cried."

"The funeral?"

"Yep. Heartbreaking scene. Well acted."

"Very well."

"Can I walk you to your car?"

I shook my head. "Terrence will be off soon. I'll wait for him."

"Can I wait with you?"

"Sure."

We sat outside on one of the benches and talked until Terrence got off work.

"Did you parents put up a fight when you decided to get emancipated?" Barry asked.

"No," I replied. "I think they threw a party after we left."

"That was harsh."

I nodded.

Chapter 33

August 6, 1991
Vancouver, Washington

I answered the ringing phone. "Hello?" I asked. "Who is it?"

"You fucking whore!" the very familiar voice bellowed.

"James?"

"Cunt! I knew you were fucking him!"

"How did you get this number?"

"Fucking bitch. Did Terrence even actually try to off himself? I bet he didn't. You and that guy got caught. Didn't you? You were fucking in the boys' room?"

"Leave me alone!"

"You'll regret this!"

I hung up and unplugged the phone. I was gonna leave it that way until it dawned on me who had told him.

Hailey must have seen us.

I plugged the phone back in and dialed my ex-best friend's phone number.

* * *

"Where did you see me and my friend at?" I demanded. "Hailey?"

"Who?" she responded.

"James just called me. He was very aggressive. Hostile. Rude. Hurtful. You gave him my number!"

"No."

"Please keep my name out of your mouth. Out of your thoughts. I used to worship you. Your freedom. Now, I despise you."

I hung up and called the phone company. I needed a new number. Pronto.

Chapter 34

A few hours later, Terrence burst through the door with Barry hot on his heels.

"What's going on?" Terrence demanded.

"What do you mean?" I asked, very confused.

"I tried called for three hours!" Barry exclaimed. He was clearly upset.

"Okay."

"When he couldn't get a hold of you, he came to the theater."

I looked at him.

"I took a chance that he was working tonight."

"So, I tried calling. When I couldn't, my boss tried, and then let me leave early."

"Wha...OH!"

"What?"

"Sorry. I had to change the number."

"Why?"

"James called. *Someone* told him about Barry and I hanging out. He was less than pleased. He had some choice words."

"Are you okay?" Barry asked.

"Who told?"

I shrugged. "Hailey? Really don't know."

"Wow."

"I'm sorry that you had to deal with that."

"I'm sorry that I worried you both. That wasn't my intention at all. I just didn't want to worry about the phone ringing and it being him. Being harassed."

"Can we get the number?"

I wrote the number down and handed it to them. "I called my job already. I was about to call yours."

"Okay."

"Did you want to stay for dinner, Barry?"

"Sure. What's for dinner?"

"Lasagna and salad."

"Great."

"I'll show you where to wash up," Terrence said.

* * *

After dinner, Terrence and Barry did the dishes and we played cards for a couple of hours.

"Are you two dating?" Terrence asked.

"No," I replied.

"You've been out a lot lately."

I nodded. "He's a friend. Barry does want more, but I'm not ready for anything else right now."

"He understands that?"

"So far. He's been very understanding and patient. I don't know if I'll ever be able to be intimate or alone with another guy again."

"Have you thought about going to therapy?"

"Of course."

He turned to look at me. "Why haven't you? Your job has insurance, right?"

"Yeah."

"Then why not?"

I sighed and took a seat on the couch we'd

purchased from Goodwill. It was a deep navy blue. We were lucky to find it in such decent condition and it had a matching love-seat and arm chairs. A true find!

"What's wrong?"

"I know that I told Barry about it, not sure why; but it's so difficult to talk about."

"Shame?"

"Yes."

Terrence took my hands. "It's not your fault. It's all James's fault."

"I know."

"Doesn't make it any easier. Please, tell me."

I thought about it. Maybe, it might help. "Okay."

"From the beginning?"

"You know the first part. School. How he was?"

"Yes."

"Somehow he'd beaten me to the house from school. He demanded that I get into his car. I almost didn't. I thought about screaming. He threatened to kill me. So, I got into the car. I buckled up and he drove us to the woods.

"Once we got there, he grilled me about Barry,
though I didn't know his name then. When I denied
his accusations and tired to explain why I was pulling
away, he backhanded me. I unbuckled and crawled
into the backseat. He came after me and ripped my
pants off, shoved me down."

I looked at Terrence. He was beyond horrified.

"He backhanded me again. Ripped my panties
off. Shoved his fingers inside of me. Then his fist.
Accused me of liking it. Accused me of being with
Hailey. Then shoved himself inside of me.

"When he was done, he pulled his clothes on
and drove to the nearest gas station. He didn't bother
to cover me up. He just left me in the backseat. Dared
me to move. I wouldn't have. I was in such pain. I was
so scared. I just stayed where he'd left me."

Terrence cleared his throat. "Then?"

My eyes welled up. "I heard when he called
Mom and Dad. He told them that he and I were going
camping. He bought some things. We went back to
the woods. He then pulled me out of the car and
threw me to the ground. Tossed me in the tent, once

it was up, and then proceeded to rape me the rest of the weekend."

Terrence started crying "What then?"

I told him some of the things he'd done to me and he screamed.

"After I got returned home, you know the rest."

Terrence took me into his arms and hugged me tightly. "I'm so sorry!" he exclaimed. "Thank you for sharing it with me. What can I do?"

I looked at him. "Help me find my daughter," I said. "I have a bad feeling."

He looked at me and said, "Of course."

Epilogue

August 15, 2001
Portland, Oregon

"Wow," I said, entering the restaurant. "They spared no expense."

"I'm surprised we were even invited," Terrence said, smiling. "We don't even know anyone."

Terrence and I arrived at a super fancy, riverside restaurant for the reunion of our graduating class. We'll the class of 1991. We didn't actually attend the graduation ceremony with them, so it was surprising.

"Thanks for inviting me," Barry said.

Barry and I had been dating off and on since

Terrence and I had become emancipated at age sixteen, and remained friendly even when we were dating.

Right now, we weren't dating, but I didn't want to show up with just my brother. Besides, Barry was fun to hand out with.

"Any time," I replied.

"Always welcome," Terrence added, smiling.

"Let's sign in."

We went to the table where all of the name tags were.

"Names?" the blond woman asked.

"Terrence and Addyson March," Terrence replied.

"Right. Graduated early."

"Yes. Do you know why we were even invited?" I asked. "I mean we didn't actually graduate with them. We never attended the ceremony since we didn't know anyone."

The woman smiled warmly. "No, but our school makes sure that everyone is included. Since your names were listed as graduates of the class of 1991, you got an invite."

"Cool. Thanks."

We took the name tags she handed us and turned to go to our table.

As we turned around, I looked up and my eyes locked with a very handsome man across the room.

No one else mattered in my life and I knew that my life would be changed for ever.

Dedication

To my husband for letting me
complain about how things
were going.

About the Author

Marie was born in Modesto, California in September of 1981 and raised in Vancouver, Washington. She graduated high school from Prairie High School in Brush Prairie, Washington in June of 2000. In January of 2006 she graduated college from Everest College (formerly Western Business College) in Vancouver, Washington.

She was raised by her maternal grandparents and has five half sisters and two half brothers.

Marie married in the fall of 2010 and they reside in Pennsylvania.

Acknowledgments

I just want to thank those of you who helped me go over this piece with a fine-tooth comb. I also want to thank my co-workers for putting up with how often I said aloud how many words I had written and how many I had left to go. Thank you for encouraging me while I wrote this!

Also enjoy these other novels from Marie Garcia

Poetry Collections

Bored and Bleeding

Egotistical Mama

Powerful Desire

From Me to You

Blood Speaks

Remembrance

Sinking Freely

Weeping Summer

Coast to Coast

Random Designs

Short Story Collections

The Scorned American

A Perfectly Secret Affair

The Haunted Third Shift

Lonely Nights and Crimson Lips

Worlds Apart and Then Some

Second Sapphire

Deadly

Key Moments

Stranded Feelings

2 in 1 Novels

Espionage Garden

Hotels Unmasked

Recreational Ballet

A Marvelous Black Death

Vacant Queen

Killer State

The Duo

The Ending

For Better or Worse

Specialty Novels

2030

Writing Death

Black Widow

Marvelous

Sai

Gypsy Rose